PEPITO THE BRAVE

PEPITO
THE BRAVE

by Scott Beck

DUTTON CHILDREN'S BOOKS · NEW YORK

Copyright © 2001 by Scott Beck

All rights reserved.

CIP Data is available.

Published in the United States by Dutton Children's Books,

a division of Penguin Putnam Books for Young Readers

345 Hudson Street, New York, New York 10014

www.penguinputnam.com

Designed by Ellen M. Lucaire

Printed in China

First Edition

1 3 5 7 9 10 8 6 4 2

ISBN 0-525-46524-3

FOR NELL

Pepito was afraid of heights.

So when it was time to leave the nest,

he decided that he would go his own way.

But how?

"You should run like me," said the fox.

So Pepito ran.

Until he came to a fence.

"When *I* come to a fence,
I hop!" said the frog.

So Pepito hopped.

It looked like smooth sailing.

Until he came to a river.

"Can you swim?" asked the fish.
"I can try."

So Pepito swam.

He was making real progress.

But then he came to a busy road.

"Why don't you fly over?" asked the gopher.
"I'm afraid of heights," said Pepito.
"Then why not go under?"

So Pepito burrowed under.

Finally, he saw his brothers'
and sisters' new tree.

He was so happy that he climbed right up.

"Pepito!" they cheered.
"How did you get here?"

"I ran, I hopped, I swam,
I burrowed, and I climbed."

His brothers and sisters
were very impressed.

"But Pepito," they said,
"if you are brave enough to
do all those things . . .

. . . then you must be brave enough to fly!"

So they all flew off . . .

and Pepito led the way.